The Ballad of the Underground Railroad

Charles L. Blockson

AuthorHouse™
1663 Liberty Drive, Suite 200
Bloomington, IN 47403
www.authorhouse.com
Phone: 1-800-839-8640

First published by AuthorHouse 4/24/2008

ISBN: 978-1-4343-5985-8 (sc)

Library of Congress Control Number: 2007910190

Printed in the United States of America
Bloomington, Indiana

This book is printed on acid-free paper.

authorHOUSE®

Introduction

The Underground Railroad is an important American story that excites men, women and children of all ages. It had the famous and unknown heroes and villains both black and white; with "stations" in 23 states and territories including linkage to Canada, Mexico and the Caribbean Islands.

William Still, a famous African American Underground Railroad agent, conductor and historian wrote in his book "The Underground Railroad:" **"men, women and children escaped from cities, plantations, rice swamps, tobacco and cotton fields, kitchens and shops, from cruel masters and owners. They were guided by the North Star alone. Penniless, braving the dangers of land and sea, eluding the keen scent of the bloodhounds, as well as the slave hunters. They were often running with nothing to call their own and a price on their heads, to a place in the North known only as the "promised land." They were dependent upon the kindness and trust of strangers known only for a fleeting moment – strangers who warmed them for a night, then shuttled the fugitive slaves on to the next station."**

No one knows how many fled from slavery in the south along the Underground Railroad's invisible tracks: As many as 100,000 between 1830 and 1860? As few as 30,000? Probably no one will ever know. The Underground Railroad or the "Freedom Train" as it was sometimes called was a secret network with coded spirituals that conveyed hidden signals. There were songs for escaping, hiding and expressing danger.

Every time I hear the spirit moving in my heart I will pray.
Jordon River it's chilly and cold. Chills the body,
but not the soul.

Upon de mountain my Lord spoke, out of his mouth came
fire and smoke.
Throughout the Underground Railroad up and down; the
Freedom Train ran for miles around.

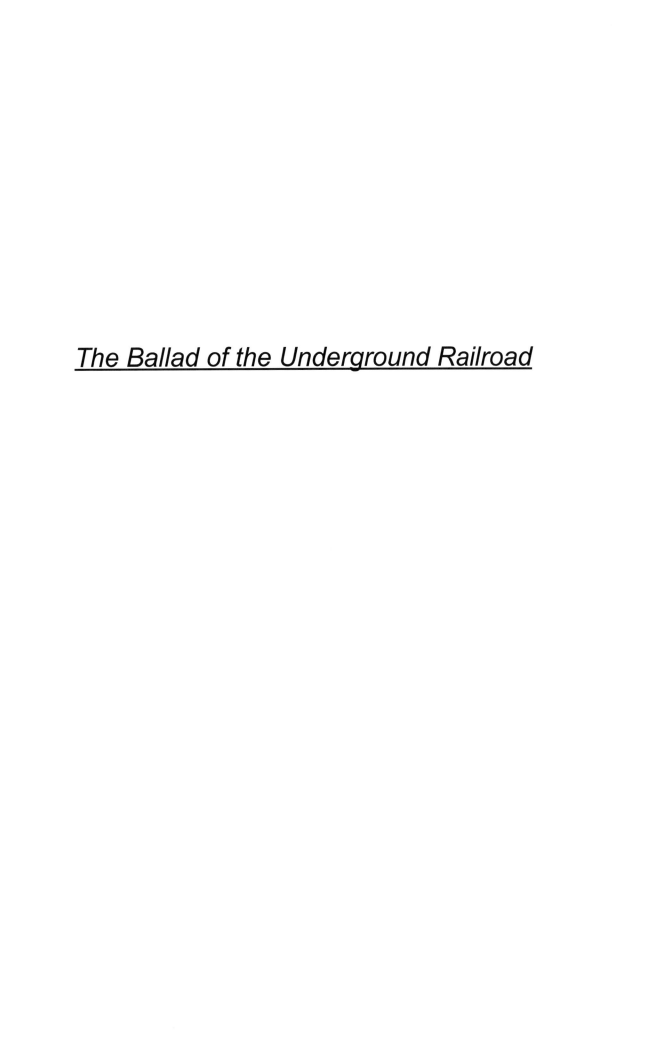

The Ballad of the Underground Railroad

The Underground Train
Strange as it seems
Carried many
passengers
And was never seen.

It wasn't made of wood
It wasn't made of steel
A man-made train that
Ran without wheels.

The train was known
By many a name
But the greatest of all
Was "The Freedom
Train."

The Quakers, the Indians,
Gentiles and Jews
Were some of the people
Who made up the crews.

Free Blacks and Christians
And Atheists, too,
Were the rest of the people
Who made up the crews.

Conductors and agents
Led the way at night
Guiding the train
By the North Star Light.

The passengers were
The runaway slaves
Running from slavery
And its evil ways.

Running from the whip
And the overseer,
From the slave block
And the auctioneer.

They didn't want their masters
To catch them again
So the men dressed as women
And the women as men.

They hid in churches,
Cellars and barns,
Waiting to hear the
Train's alarm.

Sleeping by day,
And traveling by night,
Was the best way they knew
To keep out of sight.

They waded in the waters
To hide their scent
And fool those bloodhounds
The slave masters sent.

They spoke in riddles
And sang in codes
To understand the message
You had to be told.

Those who knew the secret
Never did tell
The sacred message
Of the "Freedom Train's" bell.

Riding this train
Broke the laws of the land,

But the laws of God
       Are higher than man's.

Biography

A native of Norristown, PA, curator and emeritus of the Charles L. Blockson Afro-American Collection at Temple University; author of eleven books and recipient of three honorary degrees. He has lectured across America as well as Europe, the Caribbean, Africa and South America.

Blockson, whose relatives escaped from Delaware via the Underground Railroad with Harriet Tubman. His family has been documented in William Stills' classic book the Underground Railroad; a famous conductor and agent.

His works includes a seminal article in the National Geographic magazine July 1984, which lead to a resurgent of the interest of the Underground Railroad. He has served as chair person of the National Parks Services Underground Railroad Advisory Committee. His books includes the following: "The Underground in Pennsylvania", "First Person – Narrative of Escapees to Freedom in the North", "Hippocorean Guide to the Underground Railroad "etc.

<u>Biography</u> - <u>Artist</u>

Francine Carrie Still was born October 15, 1953 at Our Lady of Lourdes Hospital Camden, New Jersey. As a South Jersey native she has dedicated her life to the world of fine art. Majoring in art at Trenton State College and continuing her studies in commercial art at the Art Instructional School of Minneapolis, Minnesota. There she recorded the highest test score in the schools' history and was requested to expand her art studies in France. In 1985, she became a coordinator for Amnesty International and organized a community art / poetry exhibit on Human Rights at the Camden County Library. There she was recognized in the Philadelphia Inquirer. In 1992, the Camden County Board of Chosen Freeholders approached her to help launch an art project for anti-drugs and alcohol in the form of a coloring / activities book for children. The second request was for an anti-guns coloring / activities book to go throughout the South Jersey elementary schools. Both project themes were, "Just Say Nay". In 2005 painted the original cover for "The Underground Railroad" revised edition. She was invited by Bill Cosby to St. Louis, Missouri in 2006 as storyteller of her up coming book," A Girl Named Charity Still", to be read for "The Outreach Program." In the same year she taught art for the "IDEA" program for the inner city children of Camden, New Jersey. Giving back to the community where she grew up.

Her art work has been displayed at the historical Garden State Racetrack to over sized murals at the Old Firehouse in the City of Camden (Respond Program Inc.) Her work has been exhibited at the African American Museum of Philadelphia, Barnes & Noble, Smithville Mansion, Underground Railroad Museum and South Jersey Museum of American History.

"I wish to enlighten all humanity through the eyes of my soul".

F.C.S.H

Underground Railroad Glossary

Abolitionist - A person who demanded the immediate end of slavery.

Agent - A person who plotted the routes of escape for runaway slaves.

Auctioneers - A person who sold slaves to the highest bidder.

Atheist - A person who believes that there is no God.

Ballad - A short narrative poem in simple stanzas.

Bondage - The institution of slavery.

Bounty Hunter - Person seeking reward for capture of escapees.

Conductors - Persons who directly transported escaping slaves from one hiding place to another.

Enslaved Person - A group of people held in slavery.

Freedom Seeker - One who is seeking freedom while escaping.

Freedom Star - The name Harriet Tubman called the North Star.

Freedom Network - A route of travel by escapees on the Underground Railroad.

Fugitive Slaves – Freedom Seekers who escaped from the institution of slavery.

Gentile - A person who is not Jewish.

Harriet Tubman's Trail - A route of travel named for Harriet Tubman the most famous conductor on the Underground Railroad.

Night Train - A group of runaway slaves traveling together during the night.

North Star – The star of the Northern Hemisphere toward which the axis of the earth points. Other terms used in the Underground Railroad: "Big Dipper,Drinking Gourd and Freedom Star."

Overseer - A person who is in charge of a slave plantation.

Passengers - Runaway slaves who were connected with the Underground Railroad.

Promised Land - The code word for Canada where slavery was outlawed.

Station - A safe house, hiding place for escapees.

Station Master - Person in charge of a hiding place.

Underground Railroad - Formerly, a system of co-operation among certain antislavery people in the United States, whereby fugitive slaves were secretly helped to reach the North or Canada. Other names known as: "Freedom Train, Gospel Train and Lightening Train."

CPSIA information can be obtained
at www.ICGtesting.com
Printed in the USA
LVIC07080626O313
326068LV00002B

* 9 7 8 1 4 3 4 3 5 9 8 5 8 *